A NIGHT AT THE FAIR

LECTOR HOUSE PUBLIC DOMAIN WORKS

A NIGHT AT THE FAIR

FRANCIS SCOTT FITZGERALD

ISBN: 978-93-5342-061-1

First Published: 1928

LECTOR HOUSE LLP
E-MAIL: lectorpublishing@gmail.com

A NIGHT AT THE FAIR

BY

F. SCOTT FITZGERALD

1928

A NIGHT AT THE FAIR

The two cities were separated only by a thin well-bridged river; their tails curling over the banks met and mingled, and at the juncture, under the jealous eye of each, lay, every fall, the State Fair. Because of this advantageous position, and because of the agricultural eminence of the state, the fair was one of the most magnificent in America. There were immense exhibits of grain, livestock and farming machinery; there were horse races and automobile races and, lately, aeroplanes that really left the ground; there was a tumultuous Midway with Coney Island thrillers to whirl you through space, and a whining, tinkling hoochie-coochie show. As a compromise between the serious and the trivial, a grand exhibition of fireworks, culminating in a representation of the Battle of Gettysburg, took place in the Grand Concourse every night.

At the late afternoon of a hot September day two boys of fifteen, somewhat replete with food and pop, and fatigued by eight hours of constant motion, issued from the Penny Arcade. The one with dark, handsome, eager eyes was, according to the cosmic inscription in his last year's Ancient History, "Basil Duke Lee, Holly Avenue, St. Paul, Minnesota, United States, North America, Western Hemisphere, the World, the Universe." Though slightly shorter than his companion, he appeared taller, for he projected, so to speak, from short trousers, while Riply Buckner, Jr., had graduated into long ones the week before. This event, so simple and natural, was having a disrupting influence on the intimate friendship between them that had endured for several years.

During that time Basil, the imaginative member of the firm, had been the dominating partner, and the displacement effected by two feet of blue serge filled him with puzzled dismay--in fact, Riply Buckner had become noticeably indifferent to the pleasure of Basil's company in public. His own assumption of long trousers had seemed to promise a liberation from the restraints and inferiorities of boyhood, and the companionship of one who was, in token of his short pants, still a boy was an unwelcome reminder of how recent was his own metamorphosis. He scarcely admitted this to himself, but a certain shortness of temper with Basil, a certain tendency to belittle him with superior laughter, had been in evidence all afternoon. Basil felt the new difference keenly. In August a family conference had decided that even though he was going East to school, he was too small for long trousers. He had countered by growing an inch and a half in a fortnight, which added to his reputation for unreliability, but led him to hope that his mother might be persuaded, after all.

Coming out of the stuffy tent into the glow of sunset, the two boys hesitated, glancing up and down the crowded highway with expressions compounded of a certain ennui and a certain inarticulate yearning. They were unwilling to go home before it became necessary, yet they knew they had temporarily glutted their appetite for sights; they wanted a change in the tone, the motif, of the day. Near them was the parking space, as yet a modest yard; and as they lingered indecisively, their eyes were caught and held by a small car, red in color and slung at that proximity to the ground which indicated both speed of motion and speed of life. It was a Blatz Wildcat, and for the next five years it represented the ambition of several million American boys. Occupying it, in the posture of aloof exhaustion exacted by the sloping seat, was a blonde, gay, baby-faced girl.

The two boys stared. She bent upon them a single cool glance and then returned to her avocation of reclining in a Blatz Wildcat and looking haughtily at the sky. The two boys exchanged a glance, but made no move to go. They watched the girl--when they felt that their stares were noticeable they dropped their eyes and gazed at the car.

After several minutes a young man with a very pink face and pink hair, wearing a yellow suit and hat and drawing on yellow gloves, appeared and got into the car. There was a series of frightful explosions; then, with a measured tup-tup-tup from the open cut-out, insolent, percussive and thrilling as a drum, the car and the girl and the young man whom they had recognized as Speed Paxton slid smoothly away.

Basil and Riply turned and strolled back thoughtfully toward the Midway. They knew that Speed Paxton was dimly terrible--the wild and pampered son of a local brewer--but they envied him--to ride off into the sunset in such a chariot, into the very hush and mystery of night, beside him the mystery of that baby-faced girl. It was probably this envy that made them begin to shout when they perceived a tall youth of their own age issuing from a shooting gallery.

"Oh, El! Hey, El! Wait a minute!"

Elwood Leaming turned around and waited. He was the dissipated one among the nice boys of the town--he had drunk beer, he had learned from chauffeurs, he was already thin from too many cigarettes. As they greeted him eagerly, the hard, wise expression of a man of the world met them in his half-closed eyes.

"Hello, Rip. Put it there, Rip. Hello, Basil, old boy. Put it there."

"What you doing, El?" Riply asked.

"Nothing. What are you doing?"

"Nothing."

Elwood Leaming narrowed his eyes still further, seemed to give thought, and then made a decisive clicking sound with his teeth.

"Well, what do you say we pick something up?" he suggested. "I saw some pretty good stuff around here this afternoon."

Riply and Basil drew tense, secret breaths. A year before they had been shocked because Elwood went to the burlesque shows at the Star--now here he was holding the door open to his own speedy life.

The responsibility of his new maturity impelled Riply to appear most eager. "All right with me," he said heartily.

He looked at Basil.

"All right with me," mumbled Basil.

Riply laughed, more from nervousness than from derision. "Maybe you better grow up first, Basil." He looked at Elwood, seeking approval. "You better stick around till you get to be a man."

"Oh, dry up!" retorted Basil. "How long have you had yours? Just a week!"

But he realized that there was a gap separating him from these two, and it was with a sense of tagging them that he walked along beside.

Glancing from right to left with the expression of a keen and experienced frontiersman, Elwood Leaming led the way. Several pairs of strolling girls met his mature glance and smiled encouragingly, but he found them unsatisfactory--too fat, too plain or too hard. All at once their eyes fell upon two who sauntered along a little ahead of them, and they increased their pace, Elwood with confidence, Riply with its nervous counterfeit and Basil suddenly in the grip of wild excitement.

They were abreast of them. Basil's heart was in his throat. He looked away as he heard Elwood's voice.

"Hello, girls! How are you this evening?"

Would they call for the police? Would his mother and Riply's suddenly turn the corner?

"Hello, yourself, kiddo!"

"Where you going, girls?"

"Nowhere."

"Well, let's all go together."

Then all of them were standing in a group and Basil was relieved to find that they were only girls his own age, after all. They were pretty, with clear skins and red lips and maturely piled up hair. One he immediately liked better than the other--her voice was quieter and she was shy. Basil was glad when Elwood walked on with the bolder one, leaving him and Riply to follow with the other, behind.

The first lights of the evening were springing into pale existence; the afternoon crowd had thinned a little, and the lanes, empty of people, were heavy with the rich various smells of pop corn and peanuts, molasses and dust and cooking Wienerwurst and a not-unpleasant overtone of animals and hay. The Ferris wheel, pricked out now in lights, revolved leisurely through the dusk; a few empty cars of the roller coaster rattled overhead. The heat had blown off and there was the crisp stimulating excitement of Northern autumn in the air.

They walked. Basil felt that there was some way of talking to this girl, but he could manage nothing in the key of Elwood Leaming's intense and confidential manner to the girl ahead--as if he had inadvertently discovered a kinship of tastes and of hearts. So to save the progression from absolute silence--for Riply's contribution amounted only to an occasional burst of silly laughter--Basil pretended an interest in the sights they passed and kept up a sort of comment thereon.

"There's the six-legged calf. Have you seen it?"

"No, I haven't."

"There's where the man rides the motorcycle around. Did you go there?"

"No, I didn't."

"Look! They're beginning to fill the balloon. I wonder what time they start the fireworks."

"Have you been to the fireworks?"

"No, I'm going tomorrow night. Have you?"

"Yes, I been every night. My brother works there. He's one of them that helps set them off."

"Oh!"

He wondered if her brother cared that she had been picked up by strangers. He wondered even more if she felt as silly as he. It must be getting late, and he had promised to be home by half-past seven on pain of not being allowed out tomorrow night. He walked up beside Elwood.

"Hey, El," he asked, "where we going?"

Elwood turned to him and winked. "We're going around the Old Mill."

"Oh!"

Basil dropped back again--became aware that in his temporary absence Riply and the girl had linked arms. A twinge of jealousy went through him and he inspected the girl again and with more appreciation, finding her prettier than he had thought. Her eyes, dark and intimate, seemed to have wakened at the growing brilliance of the illumination overhead; there was the promise of excitement in them now, like the promise of the cooling night.

He considered taking her other arm, but it was too late; she and Riply were laughing together at something--rather, at nothing. She had asked him what he laughed at all the time and he had laughed again for an answer. Then they both laughed hilariously and sporadically together.

Basil looked disgustedly at Riply. "I never heard such a silly laugh in my life," he said indignantly.

"Didn't you?" chuckled Riply Buckner. "Didn't you, little boy?"

He bent double with laughter and the girl joined in. The words "little boy" had fallen on Basil like a jet of cold water. In his excitement he had forgotten something, as a cripple might forget his limp only to discover it when he began to run.

"You think you're so big!" he exclaimed. "Where'd you get the pants? Where'd you get the pants?" He tried to work this up with gusto and was about to add: "They're your father's pants," when he remembered that Riply's father, like his own, was dead.

The couple ahead reached the entrance to the Old Mill and waited for them. It was an off hour, and half a dozen scows bumped in the wooden offing, swayed by the mild tide of the artificial river. Elwood and his girl got into the front seat and he promptly put his arm around her. Basil helped the other girl into the rear seat, but, dispirited, he offered no resistance when Riply wedged in and sat down between.

They floated off, immediately entering upon a long echoing darkness. Somewhere far ahead a group in another boat were singing, their voices now remote and romantic, now nearer and yet more mysterious, as the canal doubled back and the boats passed close to each other with an invisible veil between.

The three boys yelled and called, Basil attempting by his vociferousness and variety to outdo Riply in the girl's eyes, but after a few moments there was no sound except his own voice and the continual bump-bump of the boat against the wooden sides, and he knew without looking that Riply had put his arm about the girl's shoulder.

They slid into a red glow--a stage set of hell, with grinning demons and lurid paper fires--he made out that Elwood and his girl sat cheek to cheek--then again into the darkness, with the gently lapping water and the passing of the singing boat now near, now far away. For a while Basil pretended that he was interested in this other boat, calling to them, commenting on their proximity. Then he discovered that the scow could be rocked and took to this poor amusement until Elwood Leaming turned around indignantly and cried:

"Hey! What are you trying to do?"

They came out finally to the entrance and the two couples broke apart. Basil jumped miserably ashore.

"Give us some more tickets," Riply cried. "We want to go around again."

"Not me," said Basil with elaborate indifference. "I have to go home."

Riply began to laugh in derision and triumph. The girl laughed too.

"Well, so long, little boy," Riply cried hilariously.

"Oh, shut up! So long, Elwood."

"So long, Basil."

The boat was already starting off; arms settled again about the girls' shoulders.

"So long, little boy!"

"So long, you big cow!" Basil cried. "Where'd you get the pants? Where'd you get the pants?"

But the boat had already disappeared into the dark mouth of the tunnel, leaving the echo of Riply's taunting laughter behind.

It is an ancient tradition that all boys are obsessed with the idea of being grown. This is because they occasionally give voice to their impatience with the restraints of youth, while those great stretches of time when they are more than content to be boys find expression in action and not in words. Sometimes Basil wanted to be just a little bit older, but no more. The question of long pants had not seemed vital to him--he wanted them, but as a costume they had no such romantic significance as, for example, a football suit or an officer's uniform, or even the silk hat and opera cape in which gentlemen burglars were wont to prowl the streets of New York by night.

But when he awoke next morning they were the most important necessity in his life. Without them he was cut off from his contemporaries, laughed at by a boy whom he had hitherto led. The actual fact that last night some chickens had preferred Riply to himself was of no importance in itself, but he was fiercely competitive and he resented being required to fight with one hand tied behind his back. He felt that parallel situations would occur at school, and that was unbearable. He approached his mother at breakfast in a state of wild excitement.

"Why, Basil," she protested in surprise, "I thought when we talked it over you didn't especially care."

"I've got to have them," he declared. "I'd rather be dead than go away to school without them."

"Well, there's no need of being silly."

"It's true--I'd rather be dead. If I can't have long trousers I don't see any use in my going away to school."

His emotion was such that the vision of his demise began actually to disturb his mother.

"Now stop that silly talk and come and eat your breakfast. You can go down and buy some at Barton Leigh's this morning."

Mollified, but still torn by the urgency of his desire, Basil strode up and down the room.

"A boy is simply helpless without them," he declared vehemently. The phrase pleased him and he amplified it. "A boy is simply and utterly helpless without them. I'd rather be dead than go away to school--"

"Basil, stop talking like that. Somebody has been teasing you about it."

"Nobody's been teasing me," he denied indignantly--"nobody at all."

After breakfast, the maid called him to the phone.

"This is Riply," said a tentative voice. Basil acknowledged the fact coldly. "You're not sore about last night, are you?" Riply asked.

"Me? No. Who said I was sore?"

"Nobody. Well, listen, you know about us going to the fireworks together tonight."

"Yes." Basil's voice was still cold.

"Well, one of those girls--the one Elwood had--has got a sister that's even nicer than she is, and she can come out tonight and you could have her. And we thought we could meet about eight, because the fireworks don't start till nine."

"What do?"

"Well, we could go on the Old Mill again. We went around three times more last night."

There was a moment's silence. Basil looked to see if his mother's door was closed.

"Did you kiss yours?" he demanded into the transmitter.

"Sure I did!" Over the wire came the ghost of a silly laugh. "Listen, El thinks he can get his auto. We could call for you at seven."

"All right," agreed Basil gruffly, and he added, "I'm going down and get some long pants this morning."

"Are you?" Again Basil detected ghostly laughter. "Well, you be ready at seven tonight."

Basil's uncle met him at Barton Leigh's clothing store at ten, and Basil felt a touch of guilt at having put his family to all this trouble and expense. On his uncle's advice, he decided finally on two suits--a heavy chocolate brown for every day and a dark blue for formal wear. There were certain alterations to be made but it was agreed that one of the suits was to be delivered without fail that afternoon.

His momentary contriteness at having been so expensive made him save carfare by walking home from downtown. Passing along Crest Avenue, he paused speculatively to vault the high hydrant in front of the Van Schellinger house, wondering if one did such things in long trousers and if he would ever do it again. He was impelled to leap it two or three times as a sort of ceremonial farewell, and was so engaged when the Van Schellinger limousine turned into the drive and stopped at the front door.

"Oh, Basil," a voice called.

A fresh delicate face, half buried under a mass of almost white curls, was turned toward him from the granite portico of the city's second largest mansion.

"Hello, Gladys."

"Come here a minute, Basil."

He obeyed. Gladys Van Schellinger was a year younger than Basil--a tranquil, carefully nurtured girl who, so local tradition had it, was being brought up to marry in the East. She had a governess and always played with a certain few girls at her house or theirs, and was not allowed the casual freedom of children in a Midwestern city. She was never present at such rendezvous as the Whartons' yard, where the others played games in the afternoons.

"Basil, I wanted to ask you something--are you going to the State Fair tonight?"

"Why, yes, I am."

"Well, wouldn't you like to come and sit in our box and watch the fireworks?"

Momentarily he considered the matter. He wanted to accept, but he was mysteriously impelled to refuse--to forgo a pleasure in order to pursue a quest that in cold logic did not interest him at all.

"I can't. I'm awfully sorry."

A shadow of discontent crossed Gladys' face. "Oh? Well, come and see me sometime soon, Basil. In a few weeks I'm going East to school."

He walked on up the street in a state of dissatisfaction. Gladys Van Schellinger had never been his girl, nor indeed anyone's girl, but the fact that they were starting away to school at the same time gave him a feeling of kinship for her--as if they had been selected for the glamorous adventure of the East, chosen together for a high destiny that transcended the fact that she was rich and he was only comfortable. He was sorry that he could not sit with her in her box tonight.

By three o'clock, Basil, reading the Crimson Sweater up in his room, began giving attentive ear to every ring at the bell. He would go to the head of the stairs, lean over and call, "Hilda, was that a package for me?" And at four, dissatisfied with her indifference, her lack of feeling for important things, her slowness in going to and returning from the door, he moved downstairs and began attending to it himself. But nothing came. He phoned Barton Leigh's and was told by a busy clerk: "You'll get that suit. I'll guarantee that you'll get that suit." But he did not believe in the clerk's honor and he moved out on the porch and watched for Barton Leigh's delivery wagon.

His mother came home at five. "There were probably more alterations than they thought," she suggested helpfully. "You'll probably get it tomorrow morning."

"Tomorrow morning!" he exclaimed incredulously. "I've got to have that suit tonight."

"Well, I wouldn't be too disappointed if I were you, Basil. The stores all close at half-past five."

Basil took one agitated look up and down Holly Avenue. Then he got his cap and started on a run for the street car at the corner. A moment later a cautious afterthought caused him to retrace his steps with equal rapidity.

"If they get here, keep them for me," he instructed his mother--a man who thought of everything.

"All right," she promised dryly, "I will."

It was later than he thought. He had to wait for a trolley, and when he reached Barton Leigh's he saw with horror that the doors were locked and the blinds drawn. He intercepted a last clerk coming out and explained vehemently that he had to have his suit tonight. The clerk knew nothing about the matter. . . . Was Basil Mr. Schwartze?

No, Basil was not Mr. Schwartze. After a vague argument wherein he tried to convince the clerk that whoever promised him the suit should be fired, Basil went dispiritedly home.

He would not go to the fair without his suit--he would not go at all. He would sit at home and luckier boys would go adventuring along its Great White Way. Mysterious girls, young and reckless, would glide with them through the enchanted darkness of the Old Mill, but because of the stupidity, selfishness and dishonesty of a clerk in a clothing store he would not be there. In a day or so the fair would be over--forever--those girls, of all living girls the most intangible, the most desirable, that sister, said to be nicest of all--would be lost out of his life. They would ride off in Blatz Wildcats into the moonlight without Basil having kissed them. No, all his life--though he would lose the clerk his position: "You see now what your act did to me"--he would look back with infinite regret upon that irretrievable hour. Like most of us, he was unable to perceive that he would have any desires in the future equivalent to those that possessed him now.

He reached home; the package had not arrived. He moped dismally about the house, consenting at half-past six to sit silently at dinner with his mother, his elbows on the table.

"Haven't you any appetite, Basil?"

"No, thanks," he said absently, under the impression he had been offered something.

"You're not going away to school for two more weeks. Why should it matter--"

"Oh, that isn't the reason I can't eat. I had a sort of headache all afternoon."

Toward the end of the meal his eye focused abstractedly on some slices of angel cake; with the air of a somnambulist, he ate three.

At seven he heard the sounds that should have ushered in a night of romantic excitement.

The Leaming car stopped outside, and a moment later Riply Buckner rang the bell. Basil rose gloomily.

"I'll go," he said to Hilda. And then to his mother, with vague impersonal reproach, "Excuse me a minute. I just want to tell them I can't go to the fair tonight."

"But of course you can go, Basil. Don't be silly. Just because--"

He scarcely heard her. Opening the door, he faced Riply on the steps. Beyond was the Leaming limousine, an old high car, quivering in silhouette against the harvest moon.

Clop-clop-clop! Up the street came the Barton Leigh delivery wagon. Clop-clop! A man jumped out, dumped an iron anchor to the pavement, hurried along the street, turned away, turned back again, came toward them with a long square box in his hand.

"You'll have to wait a minute," Basil was calling wildly. "It can't make any difference. I'll dress in the library. Look here, if you're a friend of mine, you'll wait a minute." He stepped out on the porch. "Hey, El, I've just got my--got to change my clothes. You can wait a minute, can't you?"

The spark of a cigarette flushed in the darkness as El spoke to the chauffeur; the quivering car came to rest with a sigh and the skies filled suddenly with stars.

Once again the fair--but differing from the fair of the afternoon as a girl in the daytime differs from her radiant presentation of herself at night. The substance of the cardboard booths and plaster palaces was gone, the forms remained. Outlined in lights, these forms suggested things more mysterious and entrancing than themselves, and the people strolling along the network of little Broadways shared this quality, as their pale faces singly and in clusters broke the half darkness.

The boys hurried to their rendezvous, finding the girls in the deep shadow of the Temple of Wheat. Their forms had scarcely merged into a group when Basil became aware that something was wrong. In growing apprehension, he glanced from face to face and, as the introductions were made, he realized the appalling truth--the younger sister was, in point of fact, a fright, squat and dingy, with a bad complexion brooding behind a mask of cheap pink powder and a shapeless mouth that tried ceaselessly to torture itself into the mold of charm.

In a daze he heard Riply's girl say, "I don't know whether I ought to go with you. I had a sort of date with another fellow I met this afternoon."

Fidgeting, she looked up and down the street, while Riply, in astonishment and dismay, tried to take her arm.

"Come on," he urged. "Didn't I have a date with you first?"

"But I didn't know whether you'd come or not," she said perversely.

Elwood and the two sisters added their entreaties.

"Maybe I could go on the Ferris wheel," she said grudgingly, "but not the Old Mill. This fellow would be sore."

Riply's confidence reeled with the blow; his mouth fell ajar, his hand desperately pawed her arm. Basil stood glancing now with agonized politeness at his own girl, now at the others, with an expression of infinite reproach. Elwood alone was successful and content.

"Let's go on the Ferris wheel," he said impatiently. "We can't stand here all night."

At the ticket booth the recalcitrant Olive hesitated once more, frowning and glancing about as if she still hoped Riply's rival would appear.

But when the swooping cars came to rest she let herself be persuaded in, and the three couples, with their troubles, were hoisted slowly into the air.

As the car rose, following the imagined curve of the sky, it occurred to Basil how much he would have enjoyed it in other company, or even alone, the fair twinkling beneath him with new variety, the velvet quality of the darkness that is on the edge of light and is barely permeated by its last attenuations. But he was unable to hurt anyone whom he thought of as an inferior. After a minute he turned to the girl beside him.

"Do you live in St. Paul or Minneapolis?" he inquired formally.

"St. Paul. I go to Number 7 School." Suddenly she moved closer. "I bet you're not so slow," she encouraged him.

He put his arm around her shoulder and found it warm. Again they reached the top of the wheel and the sky stretched out overhead, again they lapsed down through gusts of music from remote calliopes. Keeping his eyes turned carefully away, Basil pressed her to him, and as they rose again into darkness, leaned and kissed her cheek.

The significance of the contact stirred him, but out of the corner of his eye he saw her face--he was thankful when a gong struck below and the machine settled slowly to rest.

The three couples were scarcely reunited outside when Olive uttered a yelp of excitement.

"There he is!" she cried. "That Bill Jones I met this afternoon--that I had the date with."

A youth of their own age was approaching, stepping like a circus pony and twirling, with the deftness of a drum major, a small rattan cane. Under the cautious alias, the three boys recognized a friend and contemporary--none other than the fascinating Hubert Blair.

He came nearer. He greeted them all with a friendly chuckle. He took off his cap, spun it, dropped it, caught it, set it jauntily on the side of his head.

"You're a nice one," he said to Olive. "I waited here fifteen minutes this evening."

He pretended to belabor her with the cane; she giggled with delight. Hubert Blair possessed the exact tone that all girls of fourteen, and a somewhat cruder type of grown women, find irresistible. He was a gymnastic virtuoso and his figure was in constant graceful motion; he had a jaunty piquant nose, a disarming laugh and a shrewd talent for flattery. When he took a piece of toffee from his pocket, placed it on his forehead, shook it off and caught it in his mouth, it was obvious to any disinterested observer that Riply was destined to see no more of Olive that night.

So fascinated were the group that they failed to see Basil's eyes brighten with a ray of hope, his feet take four quick steps backward with all the guile of a gentleman burglar, his torso writhe through the parting of a tent wall into the deserted premises of the Harvester and Tractor Show. Once safe, Basil's tensity relaxed, and as he considered Riply's unconsciousness of the responsibilities presently to devolve upon him, he bent double with hilarious laughter in the darkness.

Ten minutes later, in a remote part of the fairgrounds, a youth made his way briskly and cautiously toward the fireworks exhibit, swinging as he walked a recently purchased rattan cane. Several girls eyed him with interest, but he passed them haughtily; he was weary of people for a brief moment--a moment which he had almost mislaid in the bustle of life--he was enjoying his long pants.

He bought a bleacher seat and followed the crowd around the race track, seeking his section. A few Union troops were moving cannon about in preparation for the Battle of Gettysburg, and, stopping to watch them, he was hailed by Gladys Van Schellinger from the box behind.

"Oh, Basil, don't you want to come and sit with us?"

He turned about and was absorbed. Basil exchanged courtesies with Mr. and Mrs. Van Schellinger and he was affably introduced to several other people as "Alice Riley's boy," and a chair was placed for him beside Gladys in front.

"Oh, Basil," she whispered, glowing at him, "isn't this fun?"

Distinctly, it was. He felt a vast wave of virtue surge through him. How anyone could have preferred the society of those common girls was at this moment incomprehensible.

"Basil, won't it be fun to go East? Maybe we'll be on the same train."

"I can hardly wait," he agreed gravely. "I've got on long pants. I had to have them to go away to school."

One of the ladies in the box leaned toward him. "I know your mother very well," she said. "And I know another friend of yours. I'm Riply Buckner's aunt."

"Oh, yes!"

"Riply's such a nice boy," beamed Mrs. Van Schillinger.

And then, as if the mention of his name had evoked him, Riply Buckner came suddenly into sight. Along the now empty and brightly illuminated race track came a short but monstrous procession, a sort of Lilliputian burlesque of the wild gay life. At its head marched Hubert Blair and Olive, Hubert prancing and twirling his cane like a drum major to the accompaniment of her appreciative screams of laughter. Next followed Elwood Leaming and his young lady, leaning so close together that they walked with difficulty, apparently wrapped in each other's arms. And bringing up the rear without glory were Riply Buckner and Basil's late companion, rivaling Olive in exhibitionist sound.

Fascinated, Basil stared at Riply, the expression of whose face was curiously mixed. At moments he would join in the general tone of the parade with silly guffaw, at others a pained expression would flit across his face, as if he doubted that, after all, the evening was a success.

The procession was attracting considerable notice--so much that not even Riply was aware of the particular attention focused upon him from this box, though he passed by it four feet away. He was out of hearing when a curious rustling sigh passed over its inhabitants and a series of discreet whispers began.

"What funny girls," Gladys said. "Was that first boy Hubert Blair?"

"Yes." Basil was listening to a fragment of conversation behind:

"His mother will certainly hear of this in the morning."

As long as Riply had been in sight, Basil had been in an agony of shame for him, but now a new wave of virtue, even stronger than the first, swept over him. His memory of the incident would have reached actual happiness, save for the fact that Riply's mother might not let him go away to school. And a few minutes later, even that seemed endurable. Yet Basil was not a mean boy. The natural cruelty of his species toward the doomed was not yet disguised by hypocrisy--that was all.

In a burst of glory, to the alternate strains of Dixie and The Star-Spangled Banner, the Battle of Gettysburg ended. Outside by the waiting cars, Basil, on a sudden impulse, went up to Riply's aunt.

"I think it would be sort of a--a mistake to tell Riply's mother. He didn't do any harm. He--"

Annoyed by the event of the evening, she turned on him cool, patronizing eyes.

"I shall do as I think best," she said briefly.

He frowned. Then he turned and got into the Van Schellinger limousine.

Sitting beside Gladys in the little seats, he loved her suddenly. His hand swung gently against hers from time to time and he felt the warm bond that they were both going away to school tightened around them and pulling them together.

"Can't you come and see me tomorrow?" she urged him. "Mother's going to be away and she says I can have anybody I like."

"All right."

As the car slowed up for Basil's house, she leaned toward him swiftly. "Basil--"

He waited. Her breath was warm on his cheek. He wanted her to hurry, or, when the engine stopped, her parents, dozing in back, might hear what she said. She seemed beautiful to him then; that vague unexciting quality about her was more than compensated for by her exquisite delicacy, the fine luxury of her life.

"Basil--Basil, when you come tomorrow, will you bring that Hubert Blair?"

The chauffeur opened the door and Mr. and Mrs. Van Schellinger woke up with a start. When the car had driven off, Basil stood looking after it thoughtfully until it turned the corner of the street.

Lector House believes that a society develops through a two-fold approach of continuous learning and adaptation, which is derived from the study of classic literary works spread across the historic timeline of literature records. Therefore, we aim at reviving, repairing and redeveloping all those inaccessible or damaged but historically as well as culturally important literature across subjects so that the future generations may have an opportunity to study and learn from past works to embark upon a journey of creating a better future.

This book is a result of an effort made by Lector House towards making a contribution to the preservation and repair of original ancient works which might hold historical significance to the approach of continuous learning across subjects.

HAPPY READING & LEARNING!

LECTOR HOUSE LLP
E-MAIL: lectorpublishing@gmail.com